W9-CBG-244

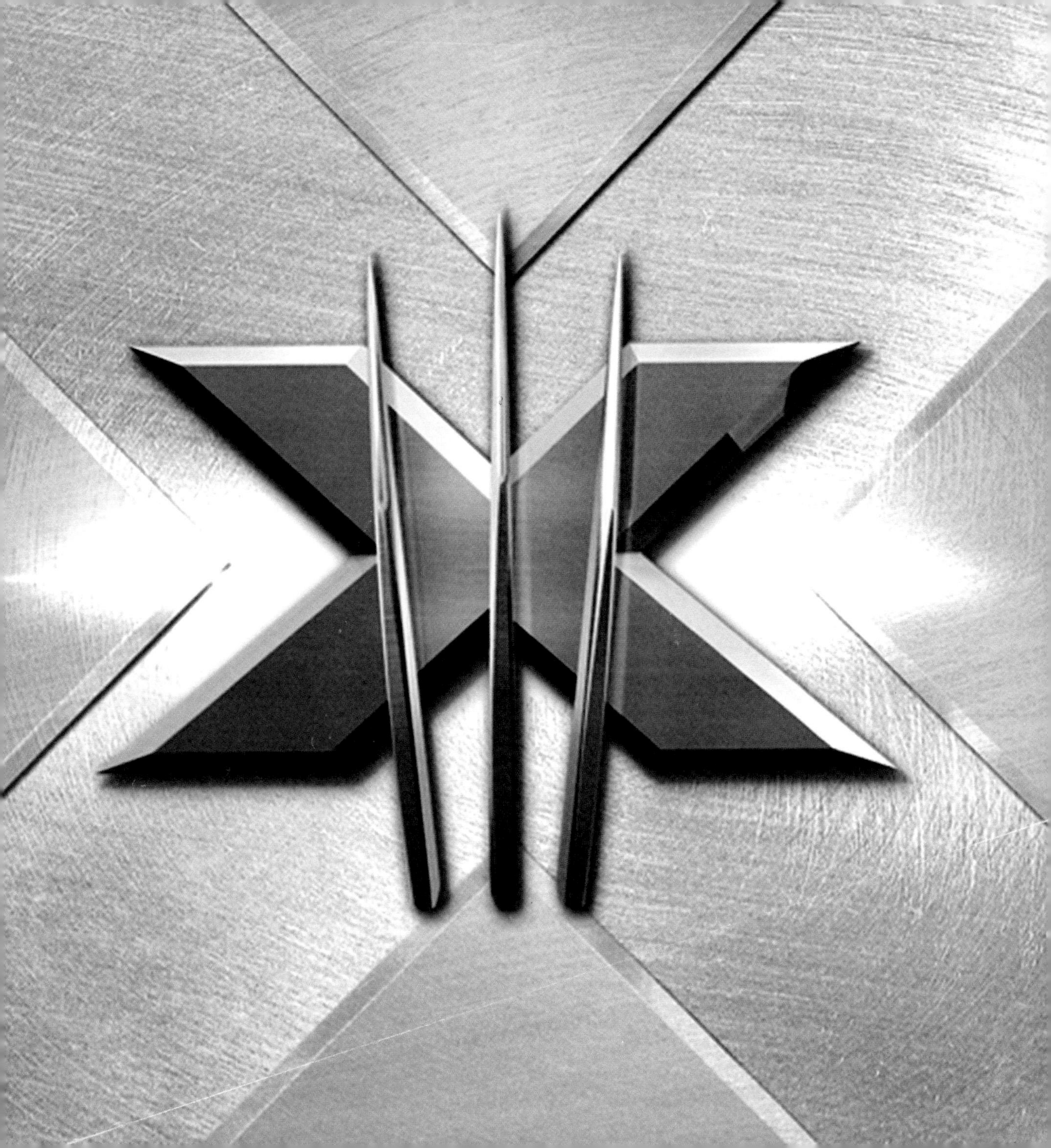

HarperCollins®, ♥®, and HarperKidsEntertainment™ are trademarks of HarperCollins Publishers.

X-Men: The Last Stand: Teaming Up
Marvel, X-Men and all related character names and the distinctive likenesses thereof are trademarks of Marvel Characters, Inc.
and are used with permission. Copyright © 2006 Marvel Characters, Inc. All rights reserved.
www.marvel.com
© 2006 Twentieth Century Fox Film Corporation
Printed in the United States of America.
No part of this book may be used or reproduced in any manner whatsoever without written permission
except in the case of brief quotations embodied in critical articles and reviews.
For information address HarperCollins Children's Books, a division of HarperCollins Publishers,
1350 Avenue of the Americas, New York, NY 10019.
www.harperchildrens.com
Book designed by John Sazaklis
Library of Congress catalog card number: 2006920160
ISBN-10: 0-06-082201-5—ISBN-13: 978-0-06-082201-9
2 3 4 5 6 7 8 9 10
❖
First Edition

TEAMING UP

Adapted By Catherine Hapka
Illustrated by Boyd Kirkland
Based on the motion picture screenplay
written by Simon Kinberg & Zak Penn

HarperKidsEntertainment
An Imprint of HarperCollinsPublishers

Wolverine and Storm were two powerful members of the X-Men team
a group of mutants trying to help mutants and humans get along.

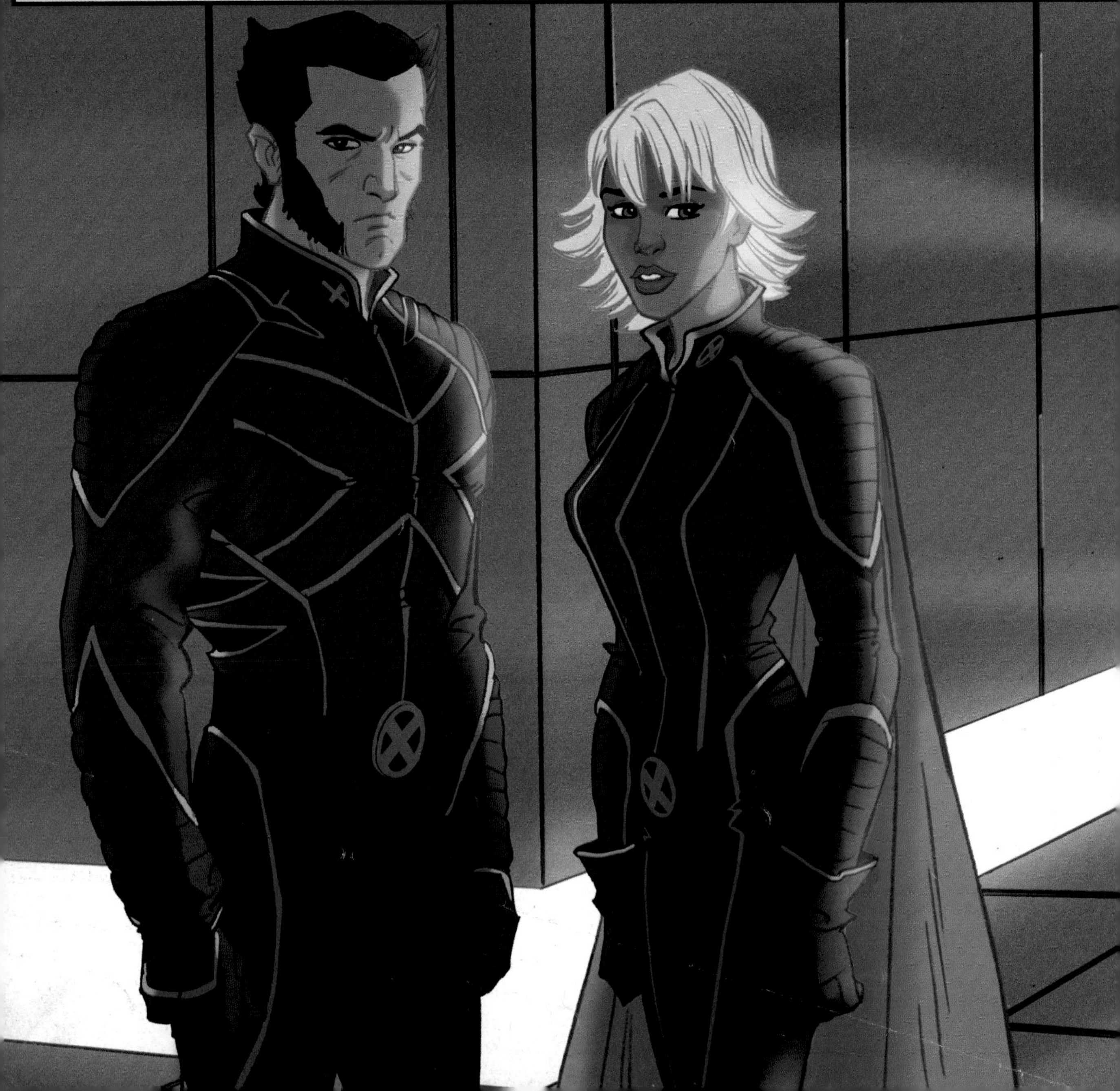

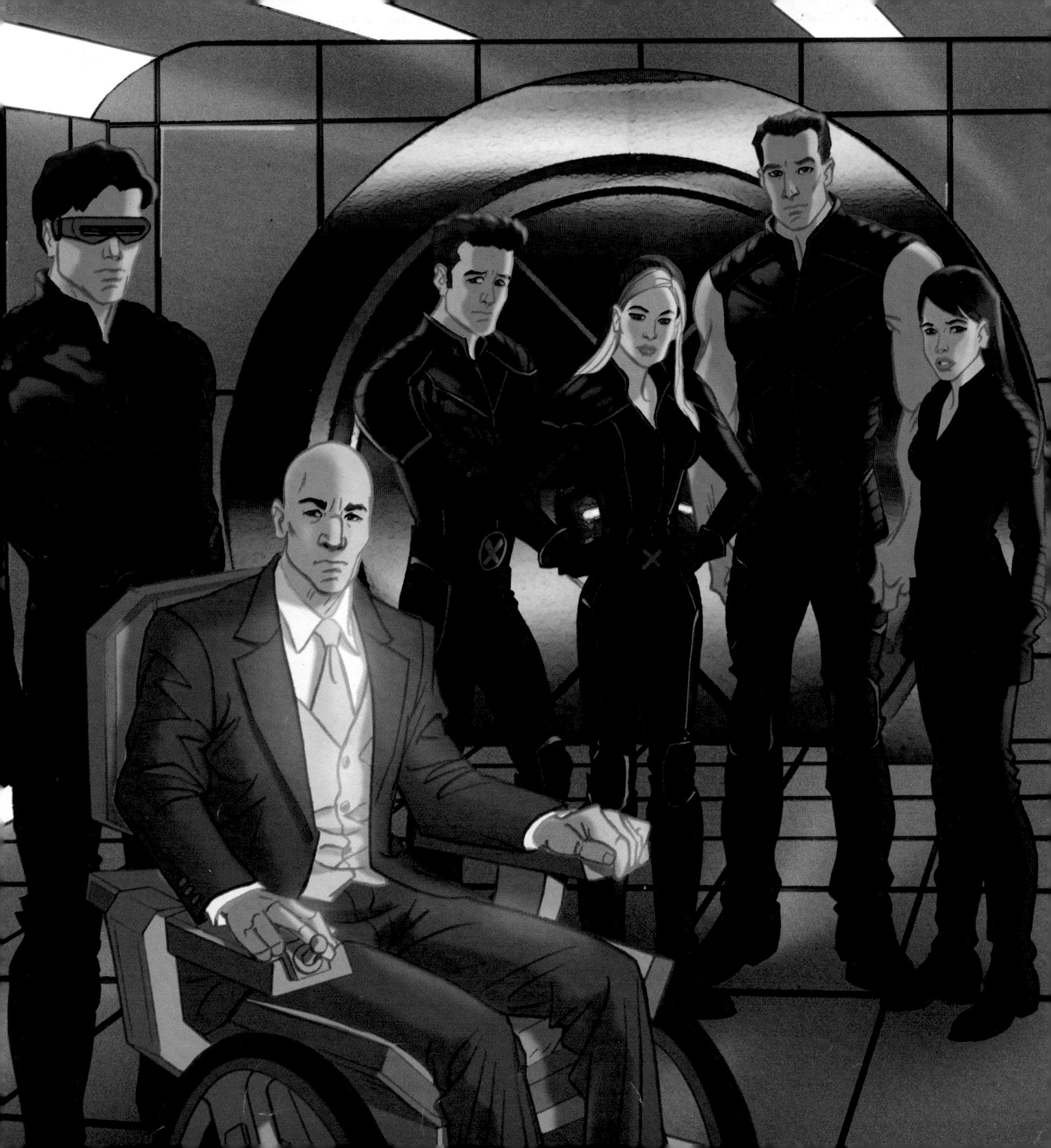

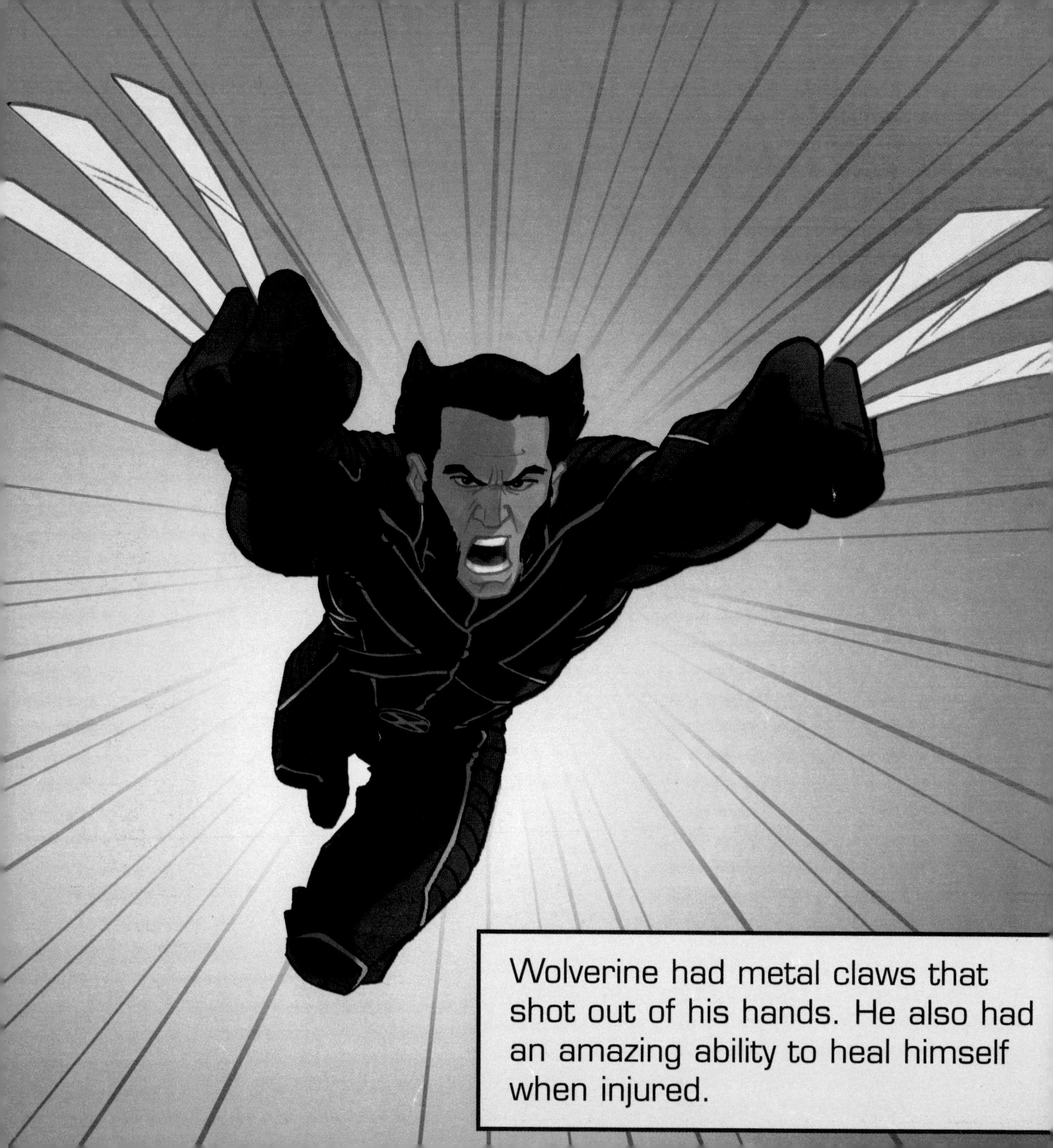

Wolverine had metal claws that shot out of his hands. He also had an amazing ability to heal himself when injured.

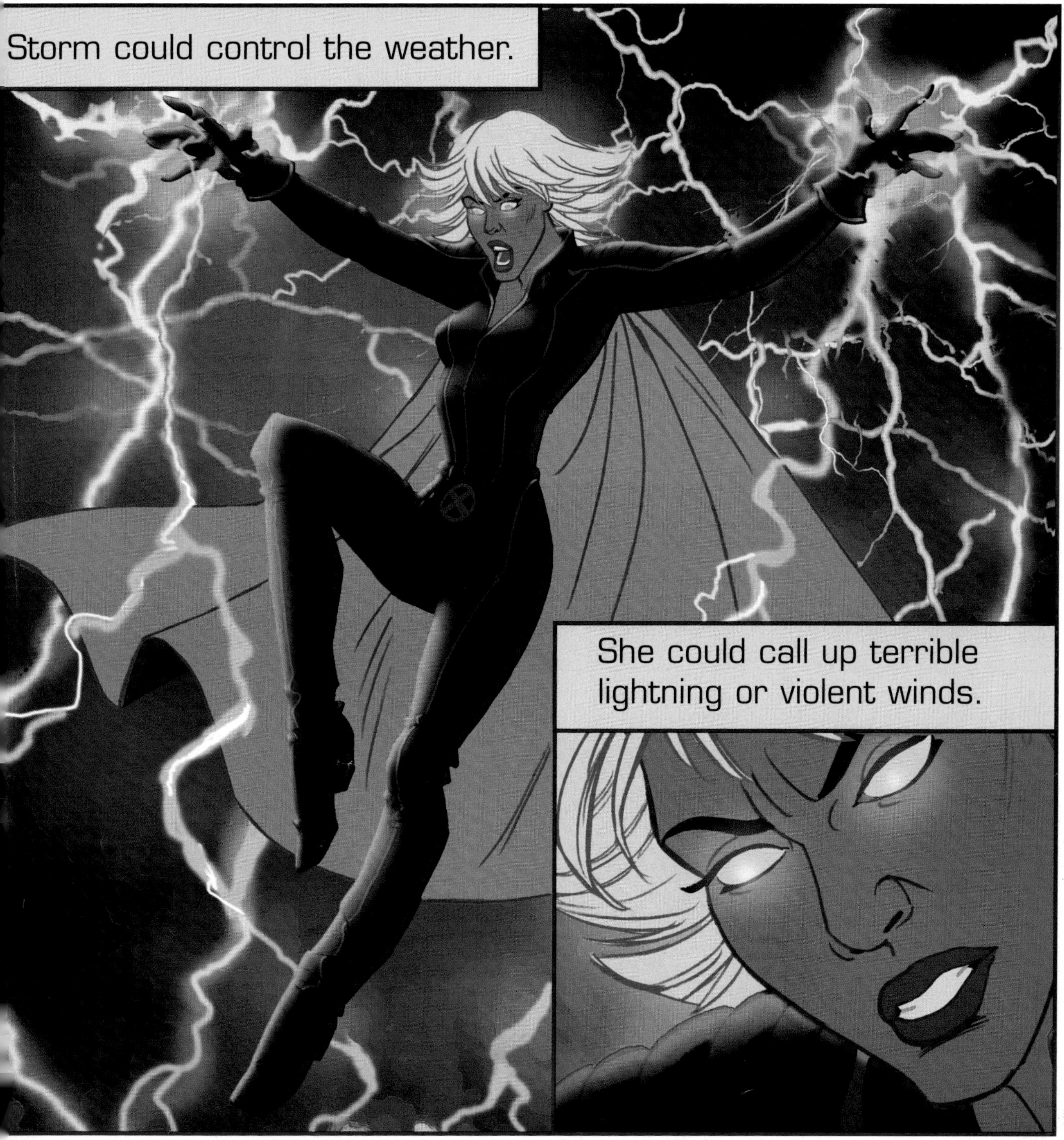
Storm could control the weather.
She could call up terrible lightning or violent winds.

Storm and Wolverine were allies. But sometimes Storm wished Wolverine would take their missions a little more seriously.

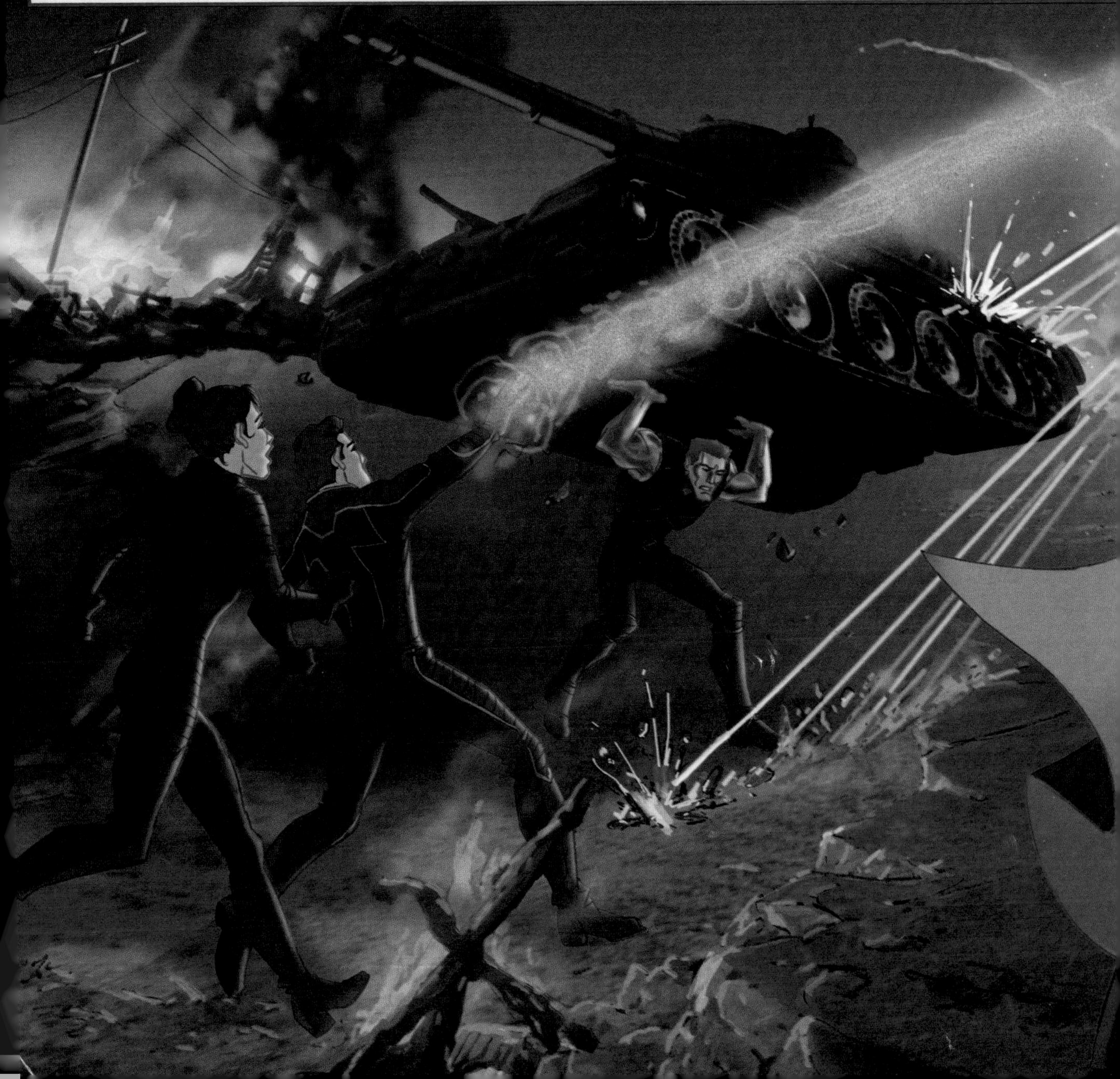

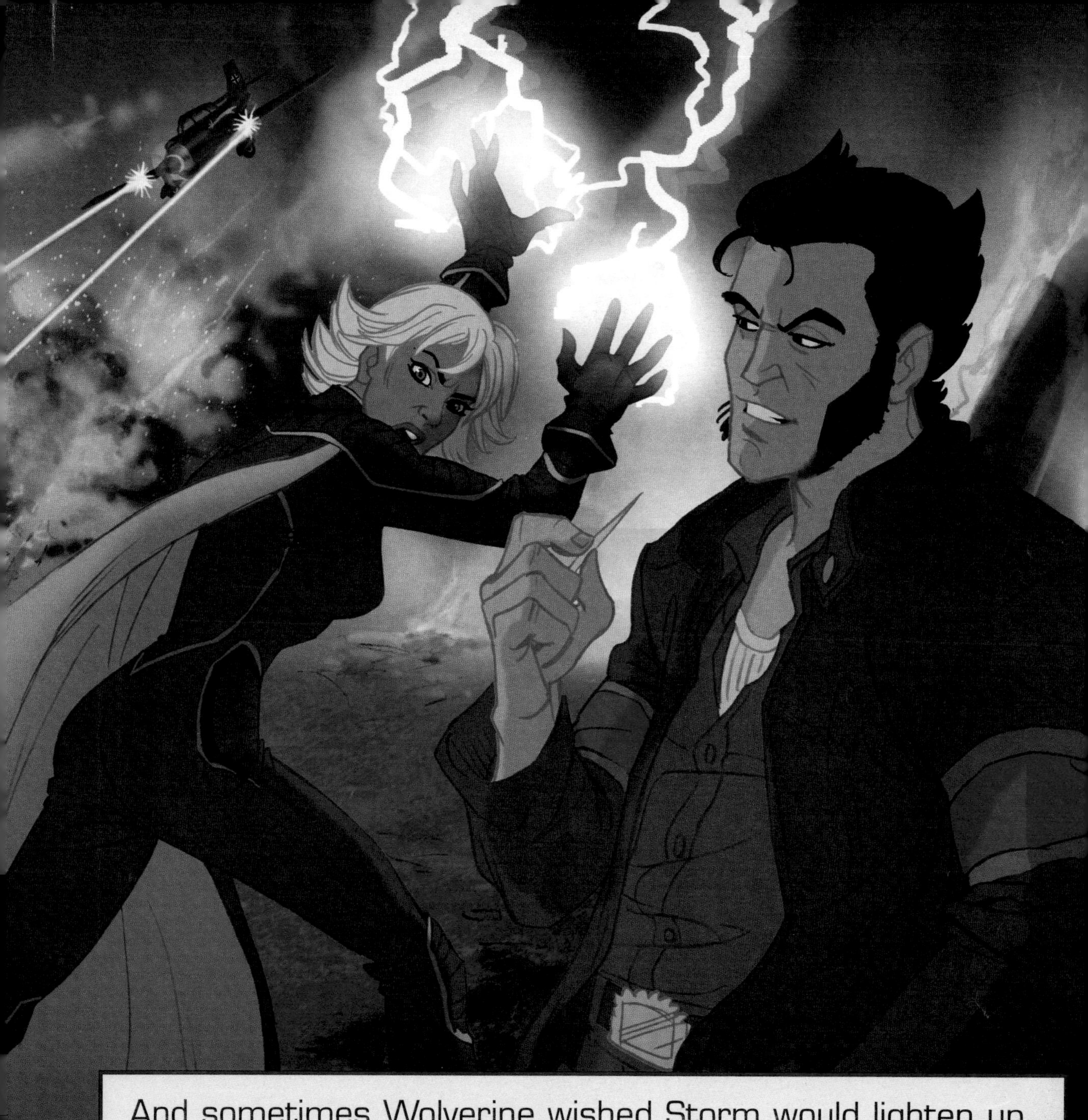

And sometimes Wolverine wished Storm would lighten up.

One day the X-Men discovered that a human scientist had created a cure—a way to fix the gene that made them all mutants.

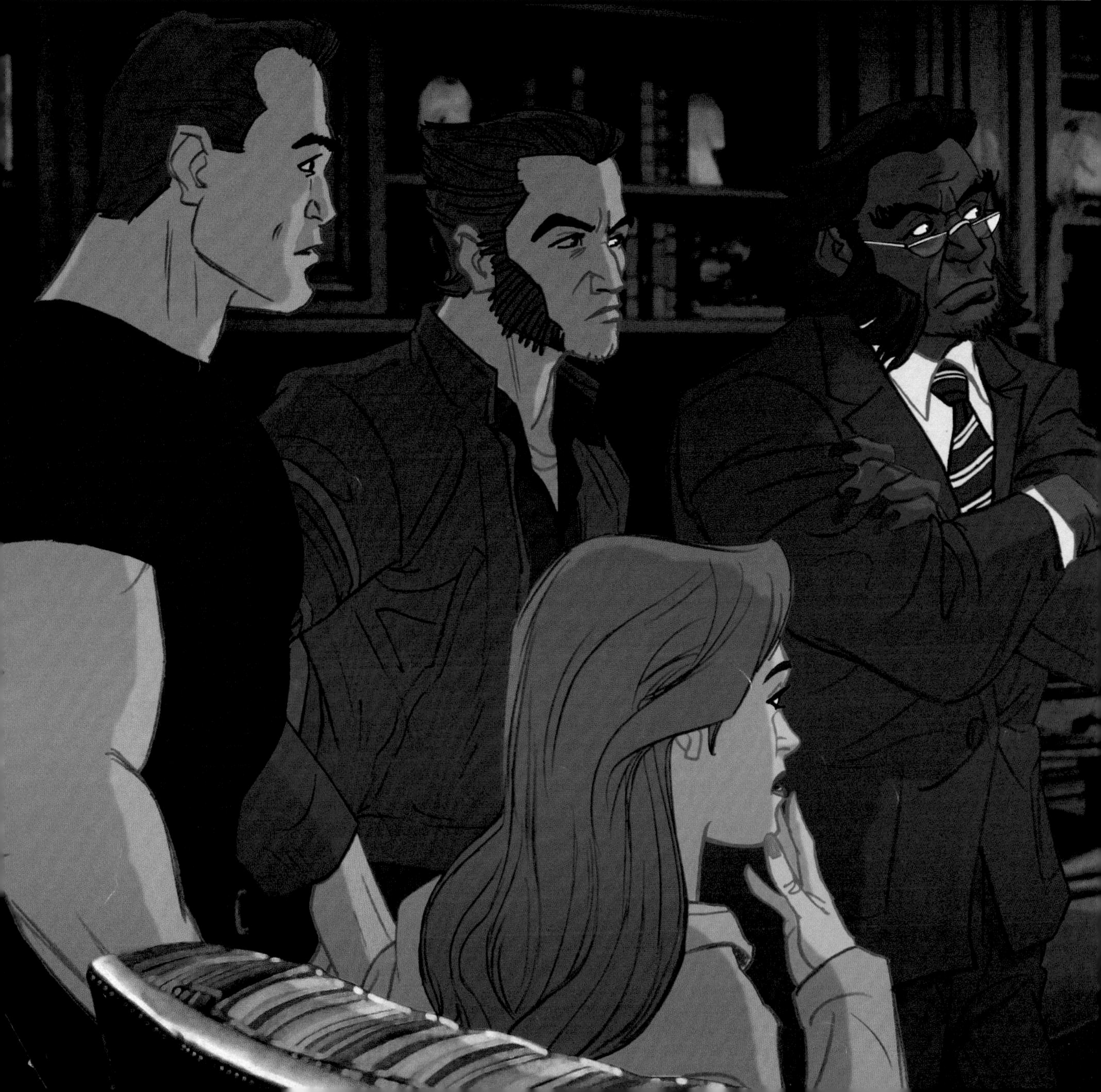

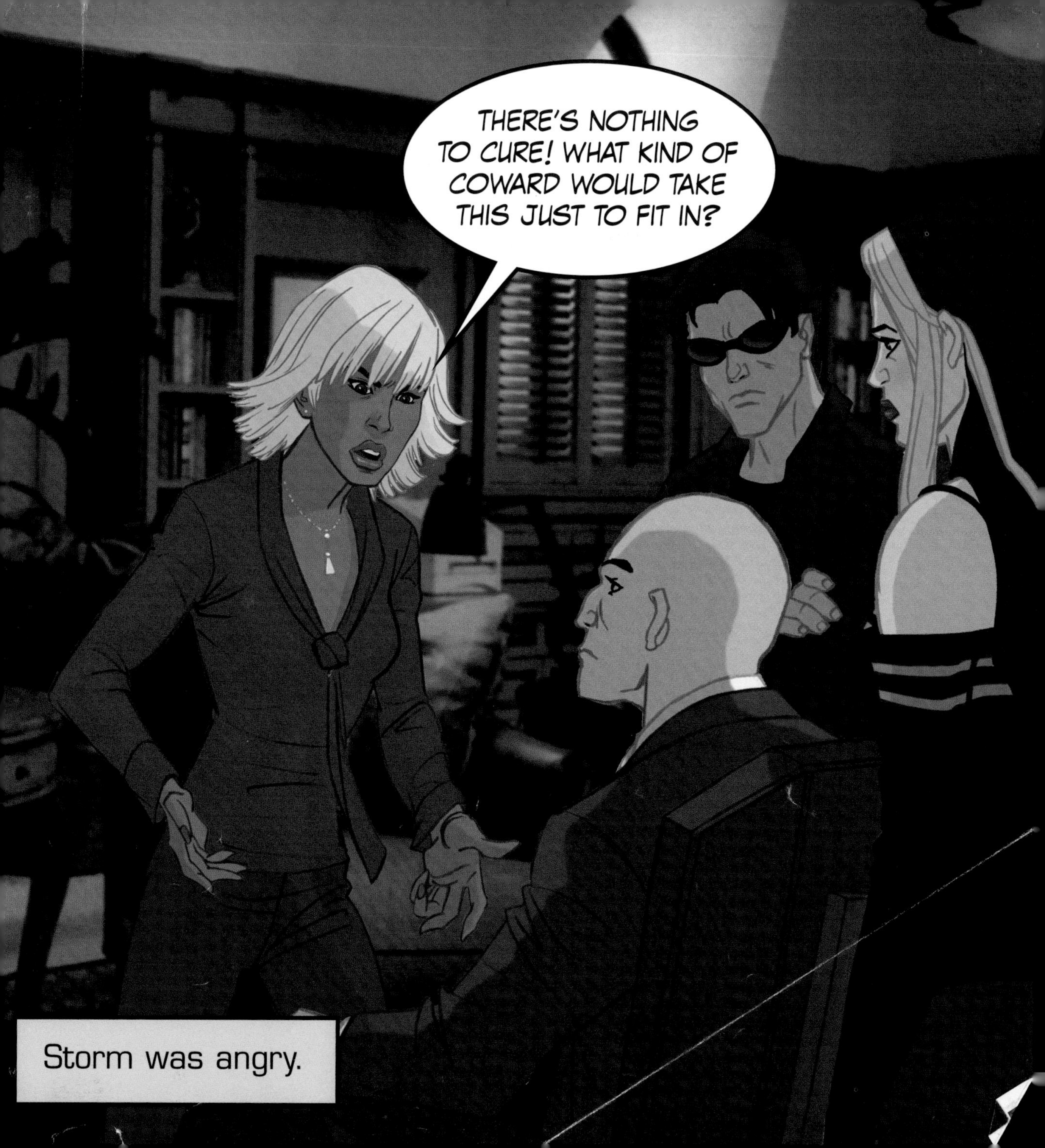
THERE'S NOTHING TO CURE! WHAT KIND OF COWARD WOULD TAKE THIS JUST TO FIT IN?

Storm was angry.

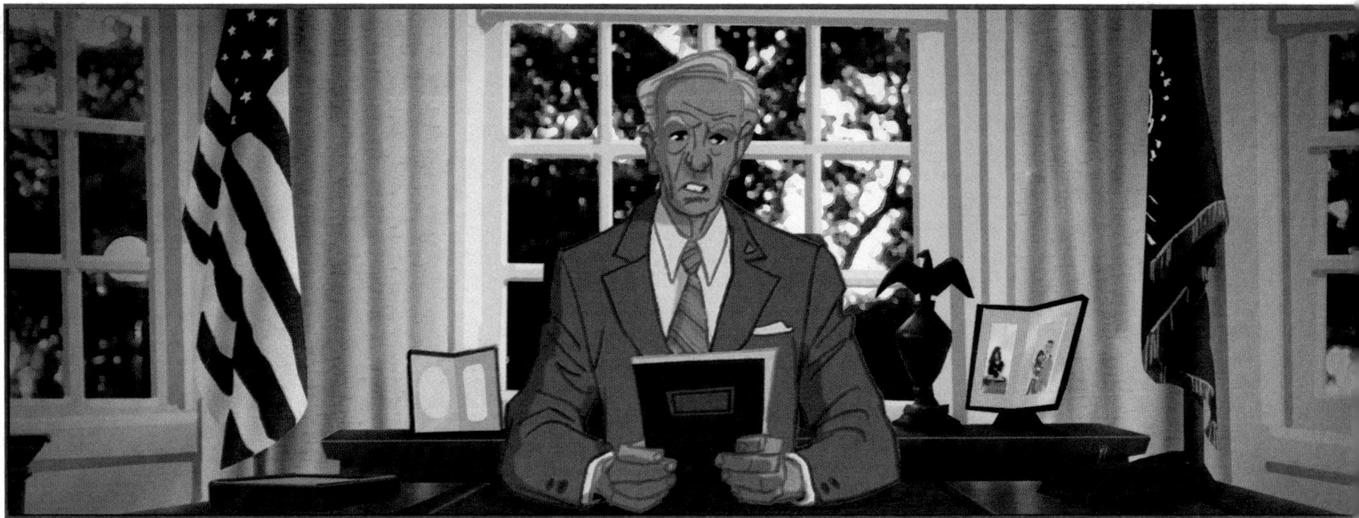

The U.S. president told everyone that the mutant cure was voluntary. But many mutants were worried: Would they be forced to give up their powers and become ordinary?

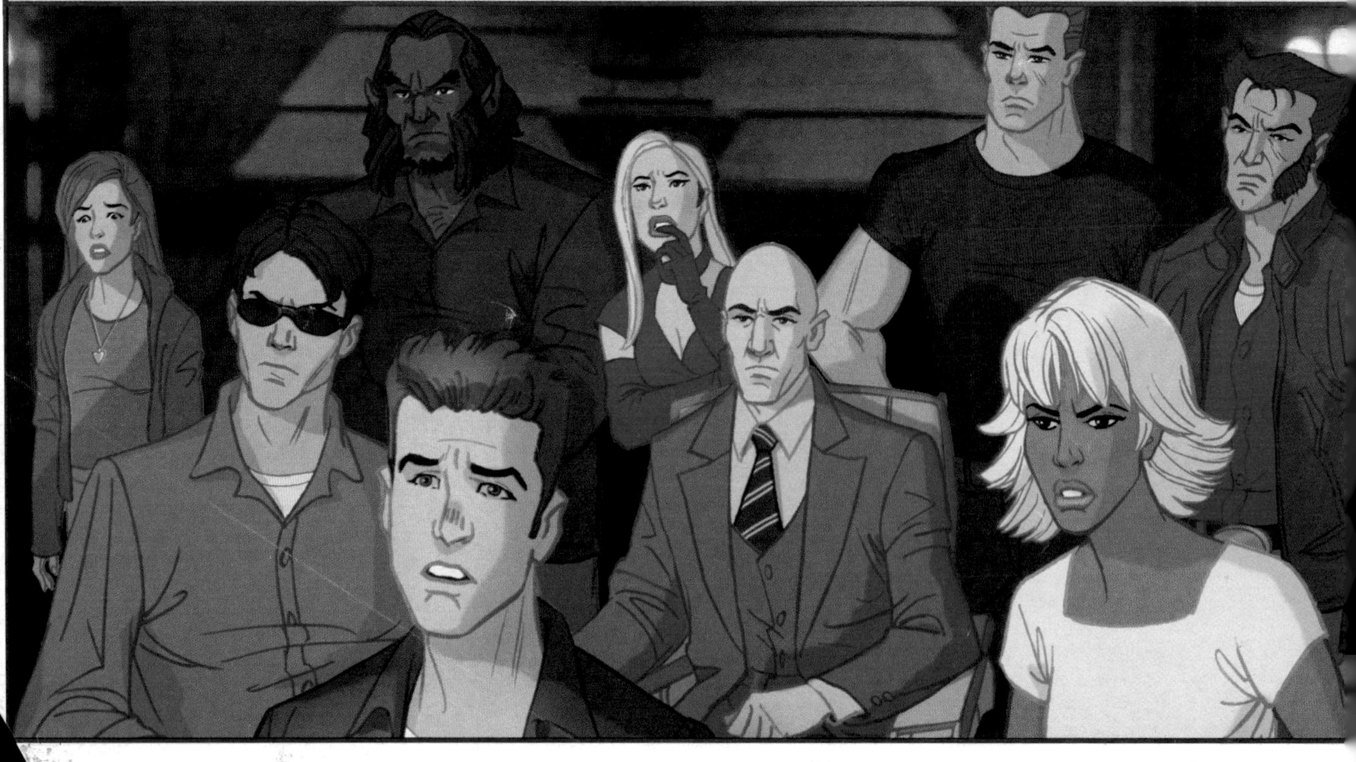

Meanwhile Storm and Wolverine found themselves working together more and more.

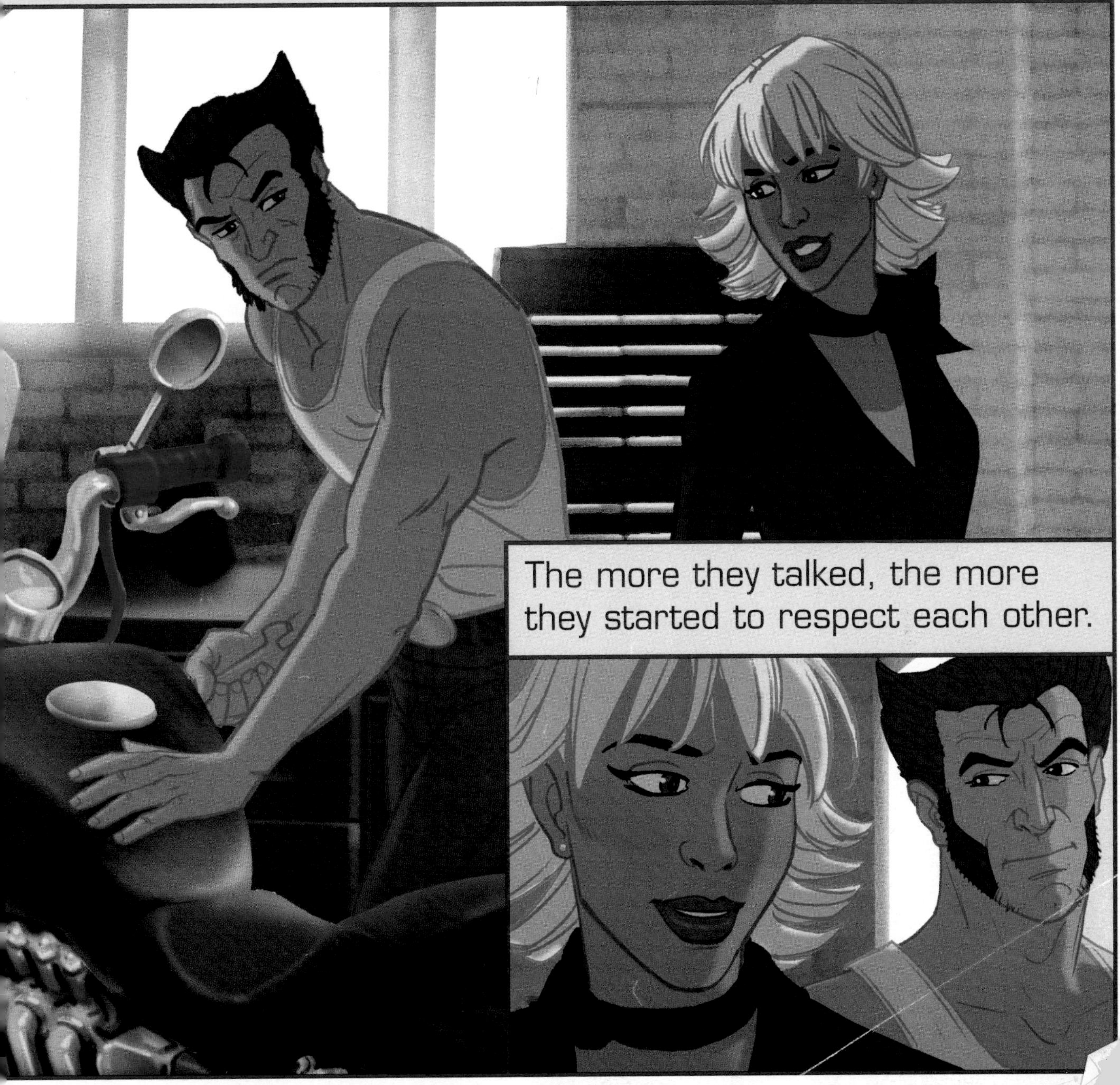
The more they talked, the more they started to respect each other.

A powerful mutant named Magneto was the archenemy of the X-Men. He convinced many of his fellow mutants that the humans wanted to harm them with their cure.

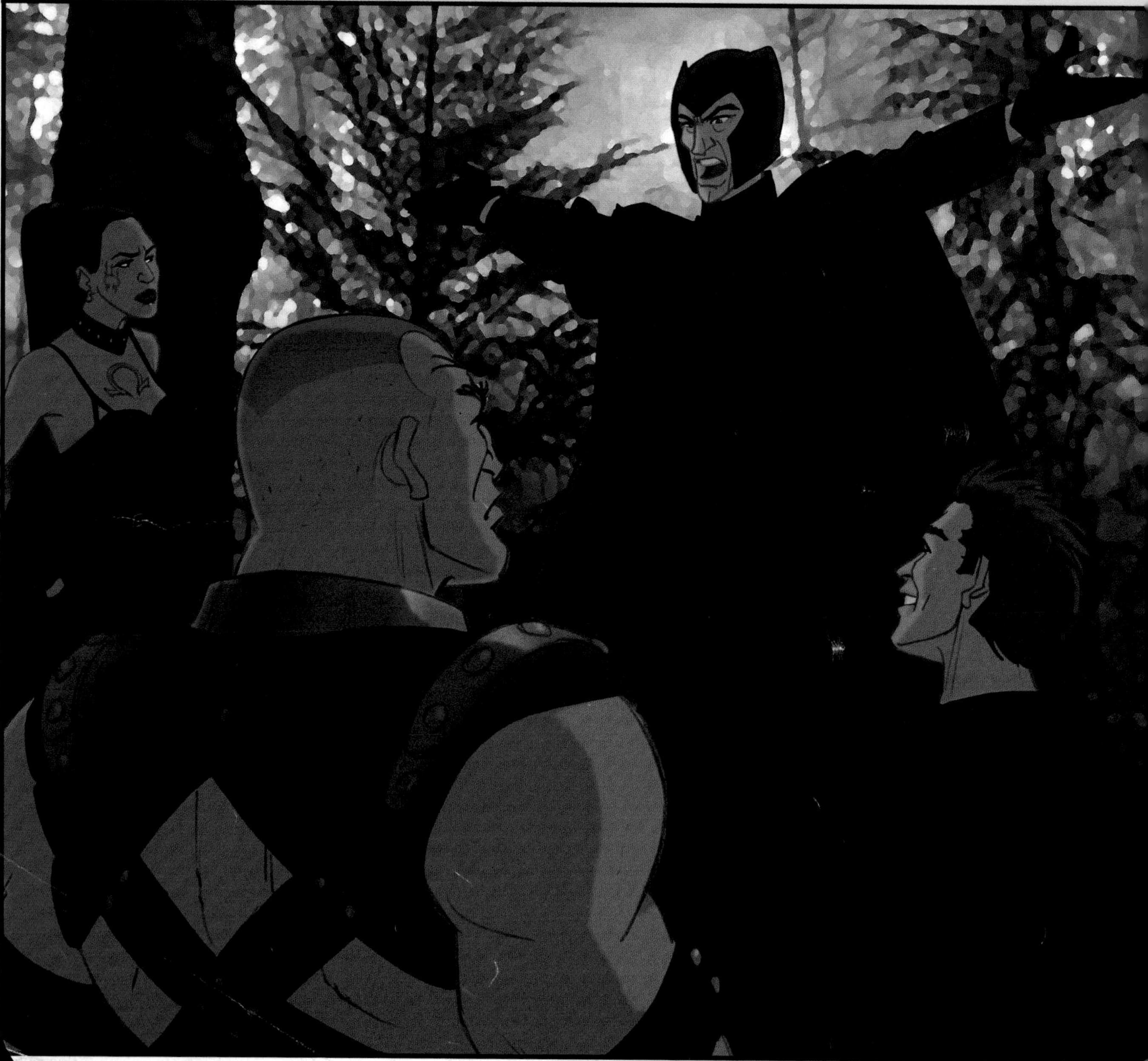

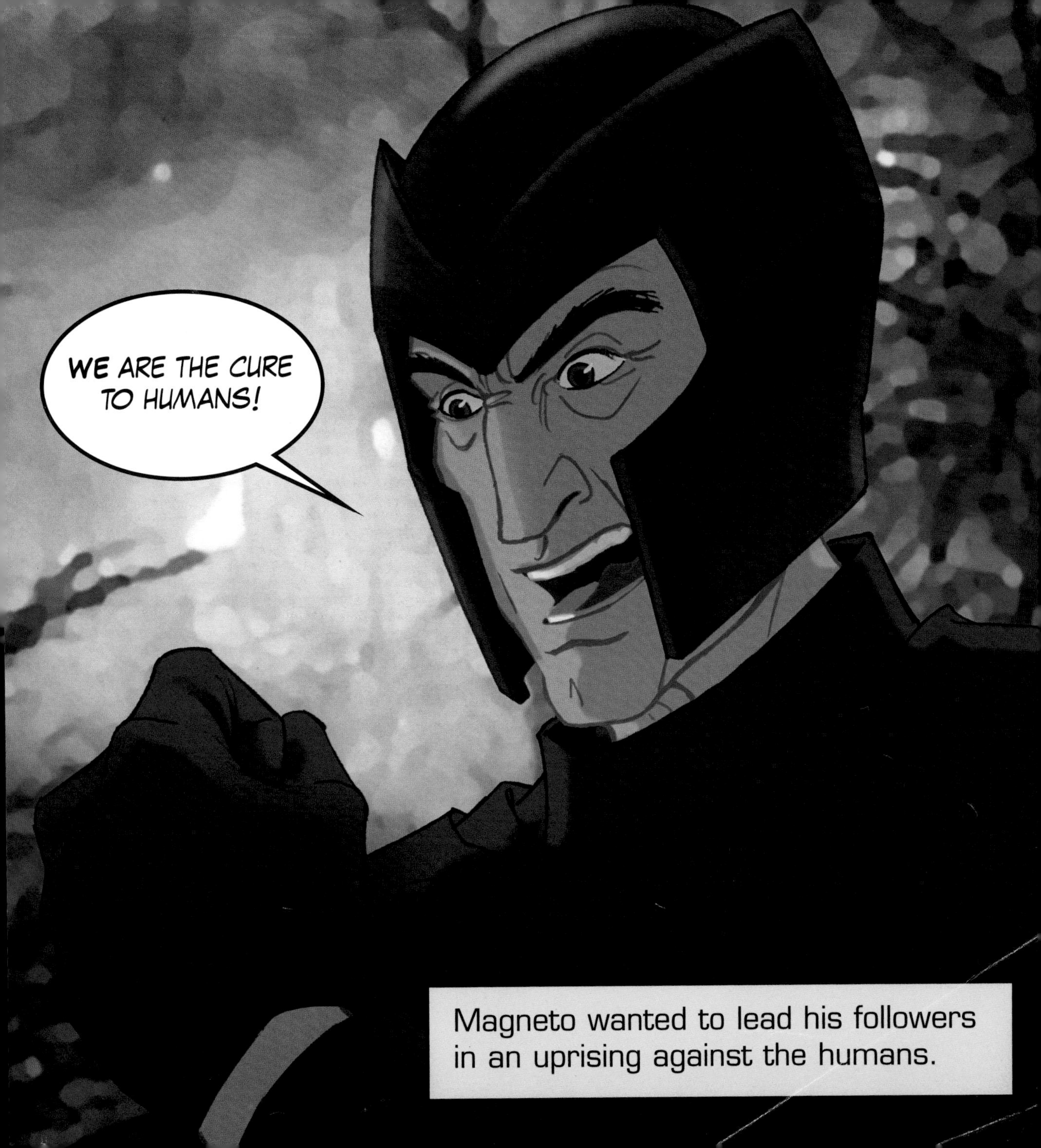
WE ARE THE CURE TO HUMANS!
Magneto wanted to lead his followers in an uprising against the humans.

The X-Men were having a different problem. One of their members, Jean Grey, was losing control of her powers. The X-Men went to her house, wanting to help her. Professor Xavier, the leader of the X-Men, went inside.

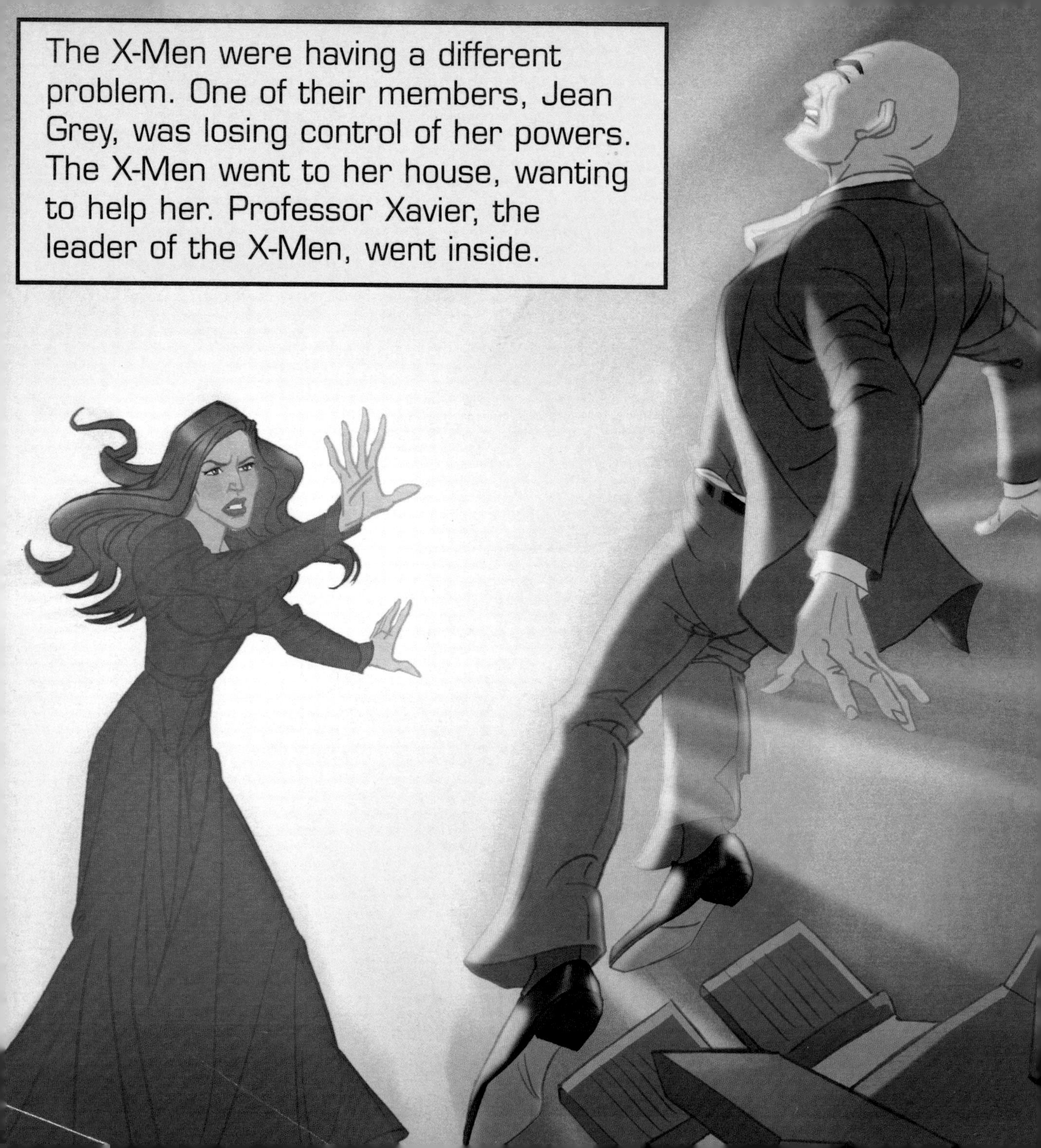

Wolverine wanted to go with him. But Storm held him back.

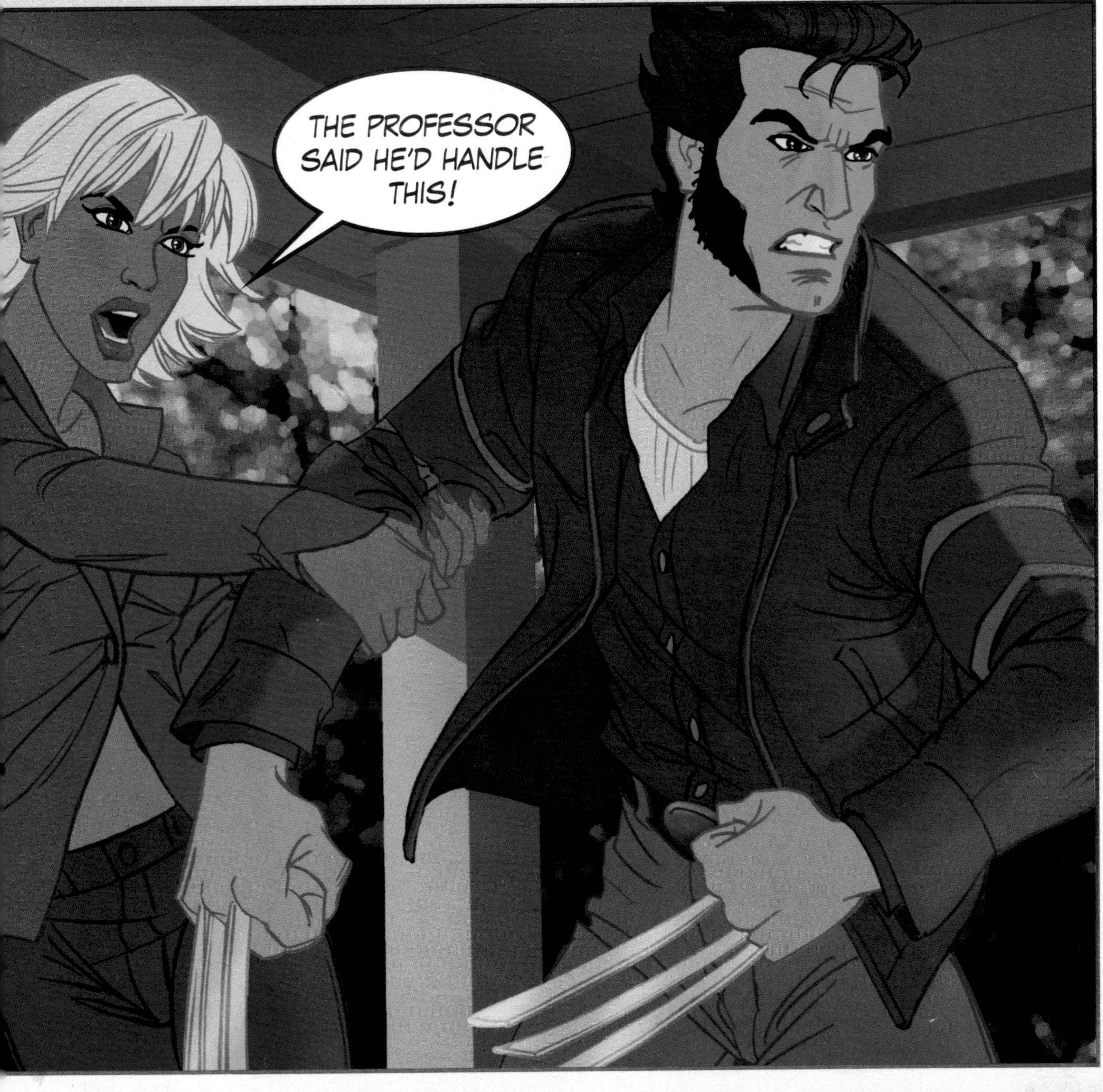
THE PROFESSOR SAID HE'D HANDLE THIS!

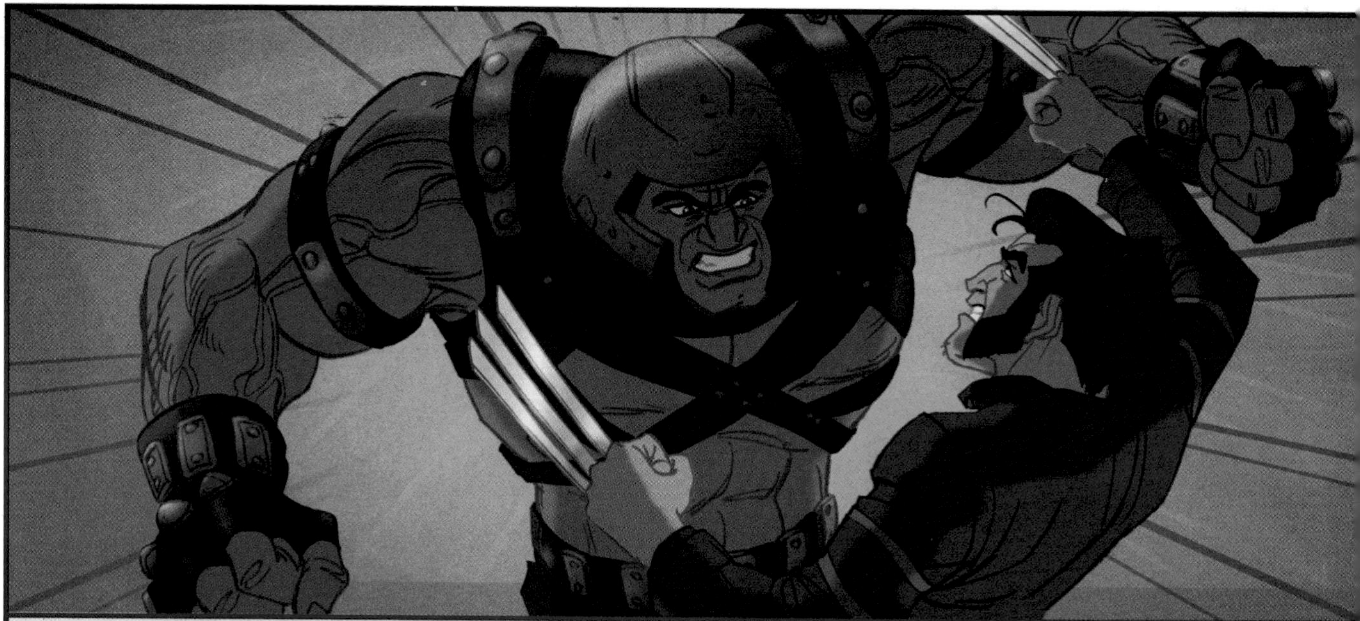

Magneto heard about Jean's powers. He and his followers went to her house, too. There they attacked Storm and Wolverine. Storm and Wolverine survived the attack. But Xavier didn't survive his meeting with Jean . . .

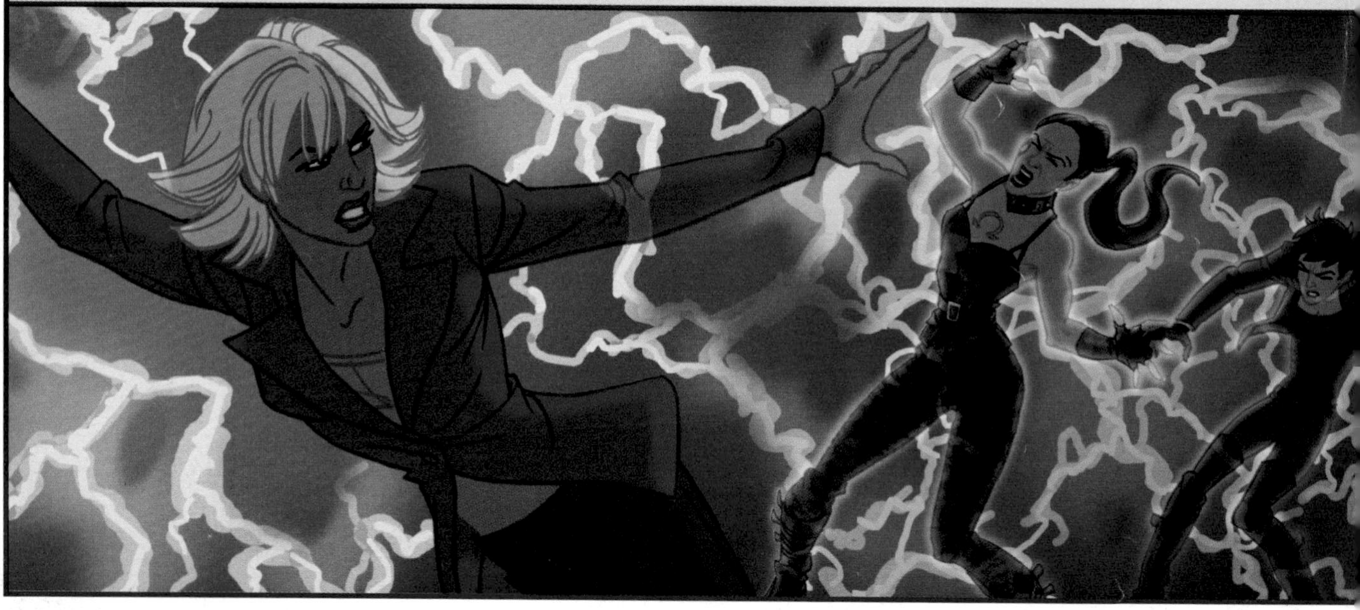

o left with Magneto.

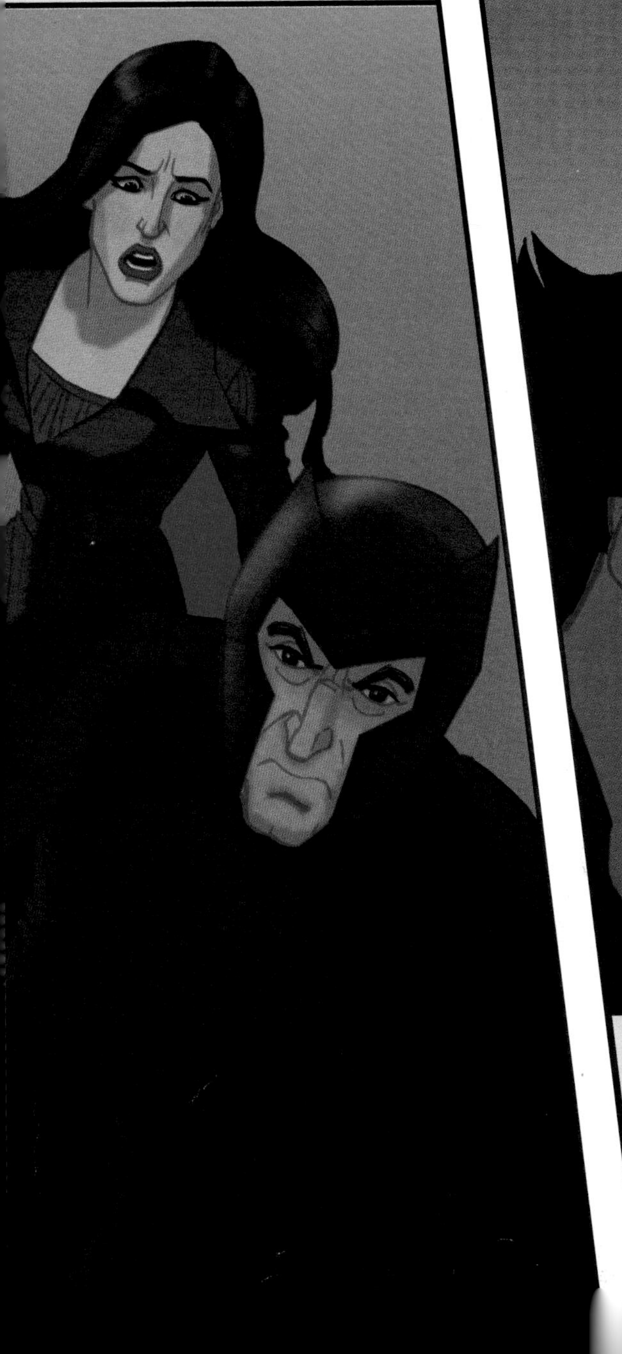

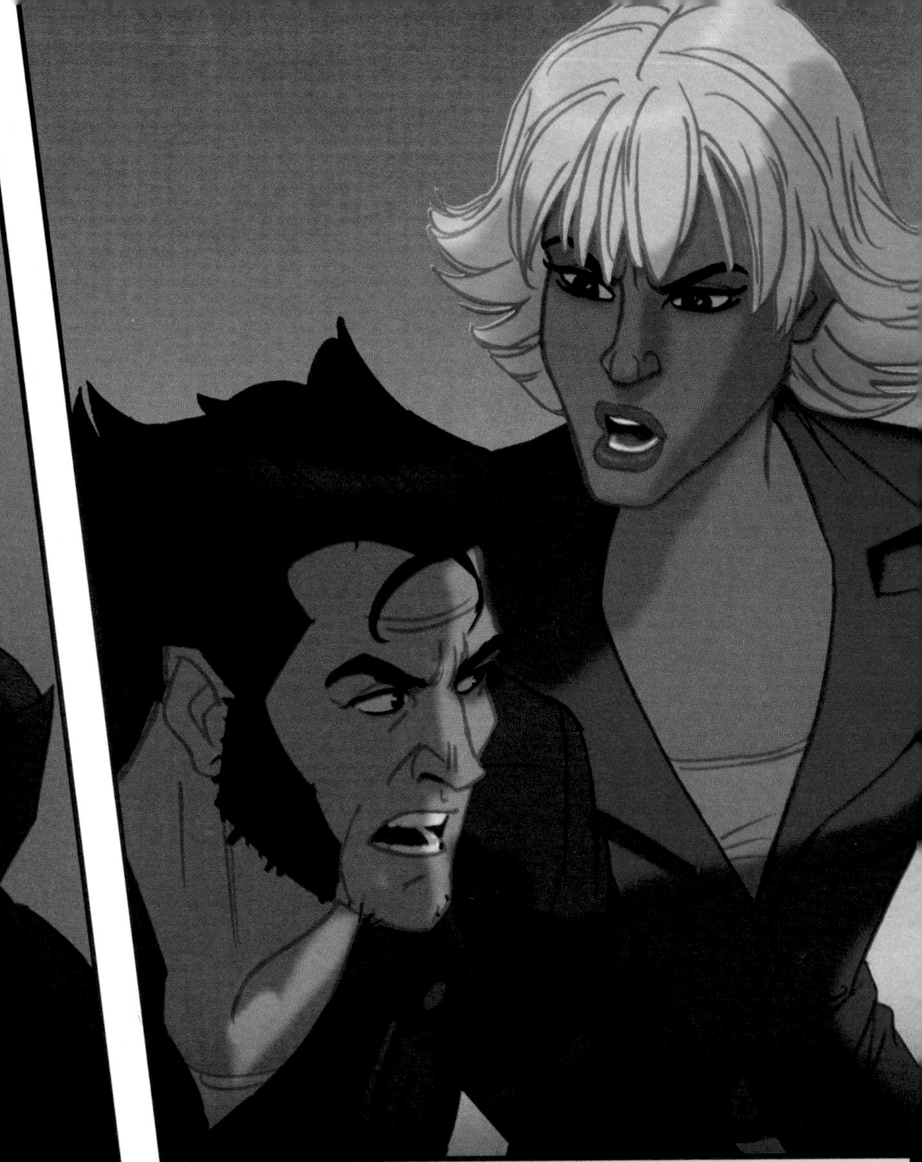

Storm and Wolverine argued about what to do next. Wolverine still wanted to try to help Jean. But Storm was afraid the new Jean was too powerful.

Wolverine tried to go after Jean on his own. But Magneto had other ideas. Still, Wolverine was ready to try again.

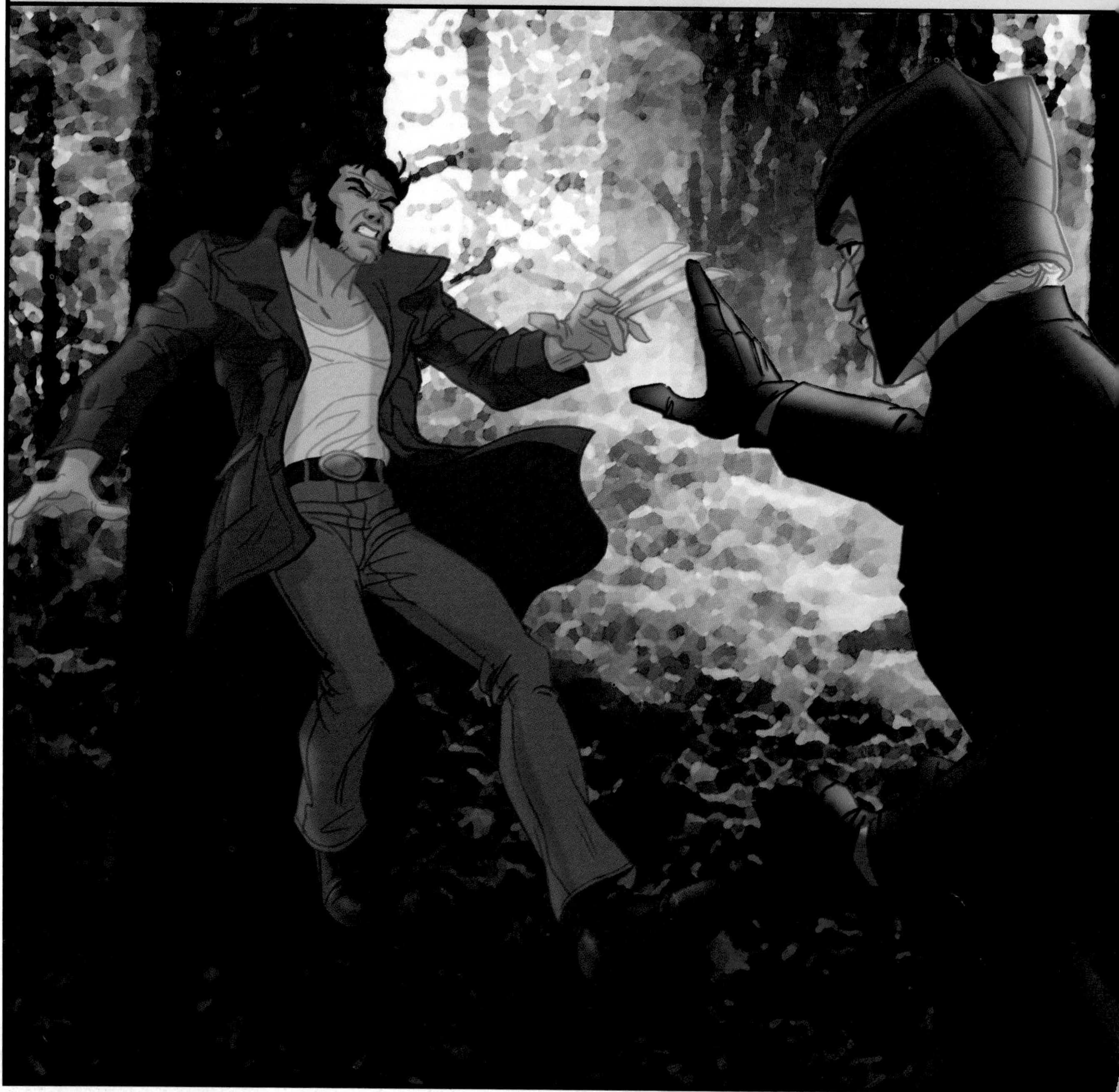

When he returned to the school to get the X-Jet, he found the other X-Men waiting for him—led by Storm.

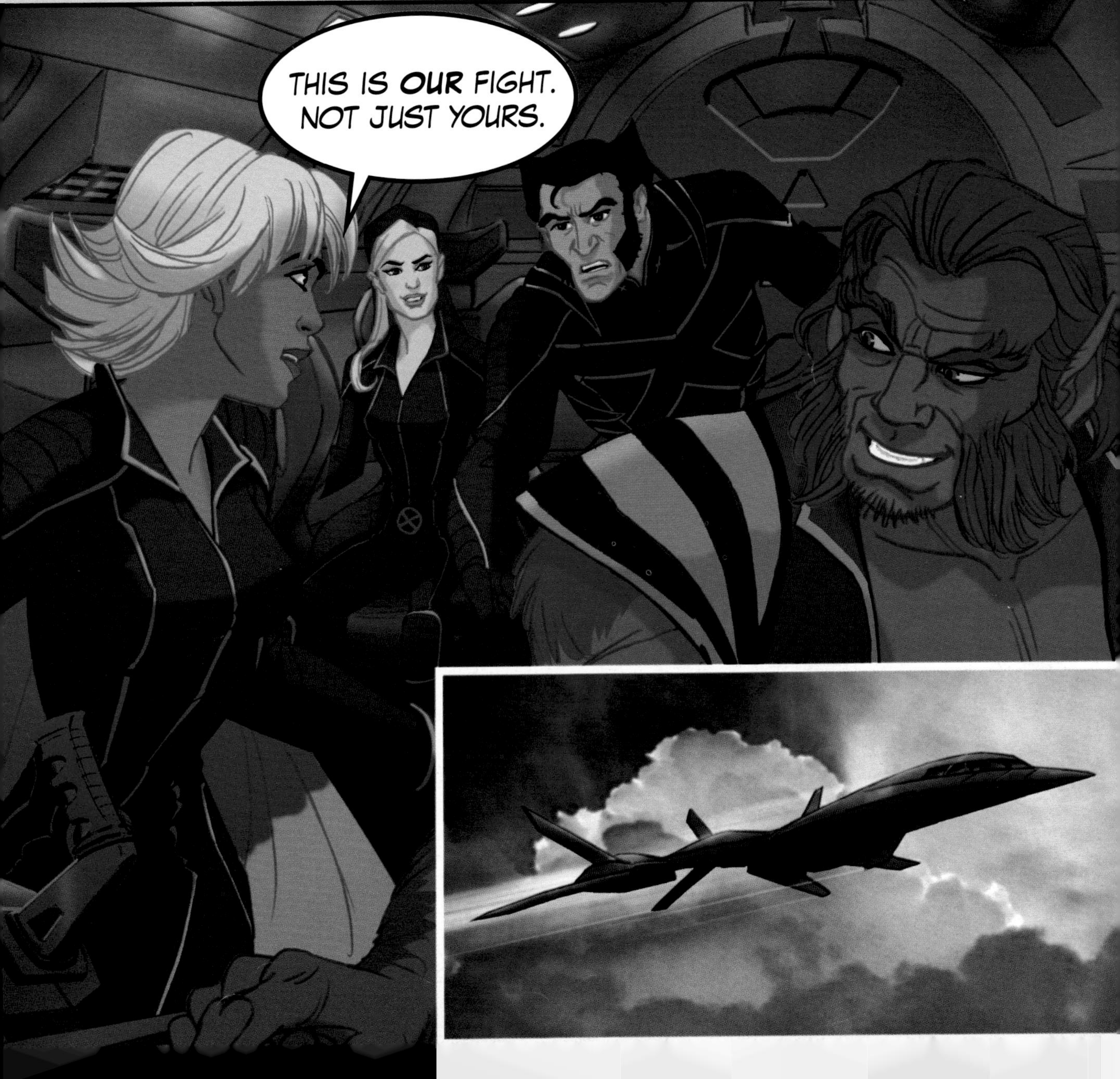
THIS IS **OUR** FIGHT. NOT JUST YOURS.

The X-Men flew to join the battle raging at the human lab where the cure was made.

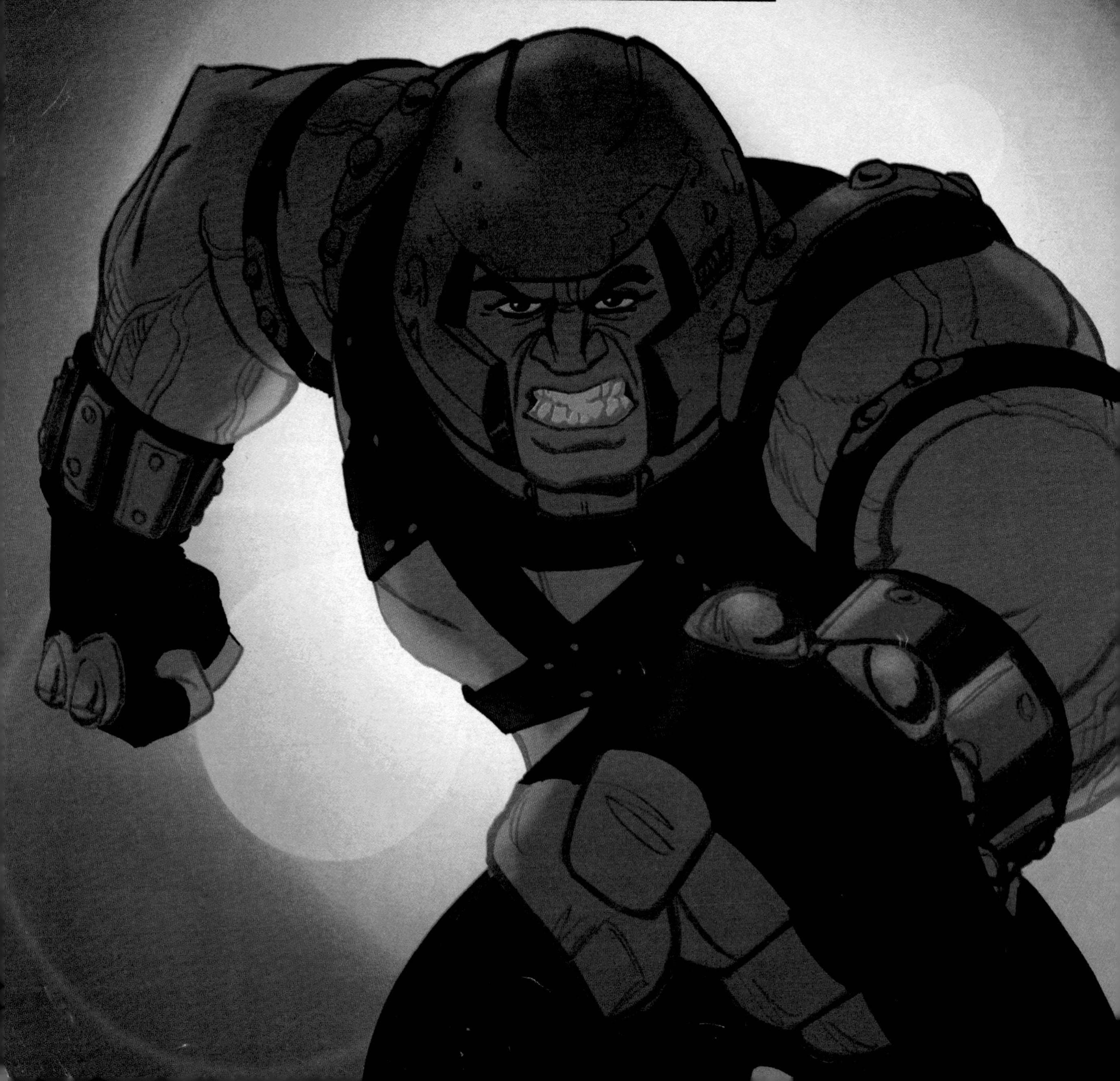

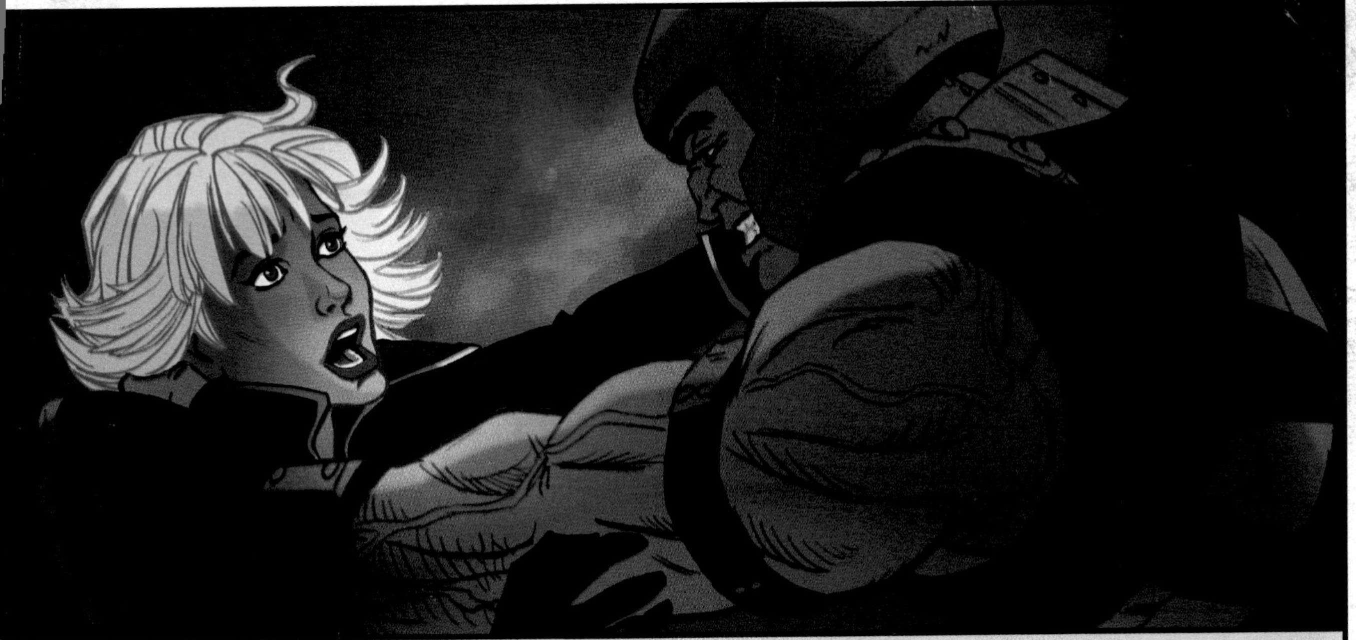

Magneto's forces were strong, but when they joined their powers together and worked as a team, Storm and Wolverine were stronger.

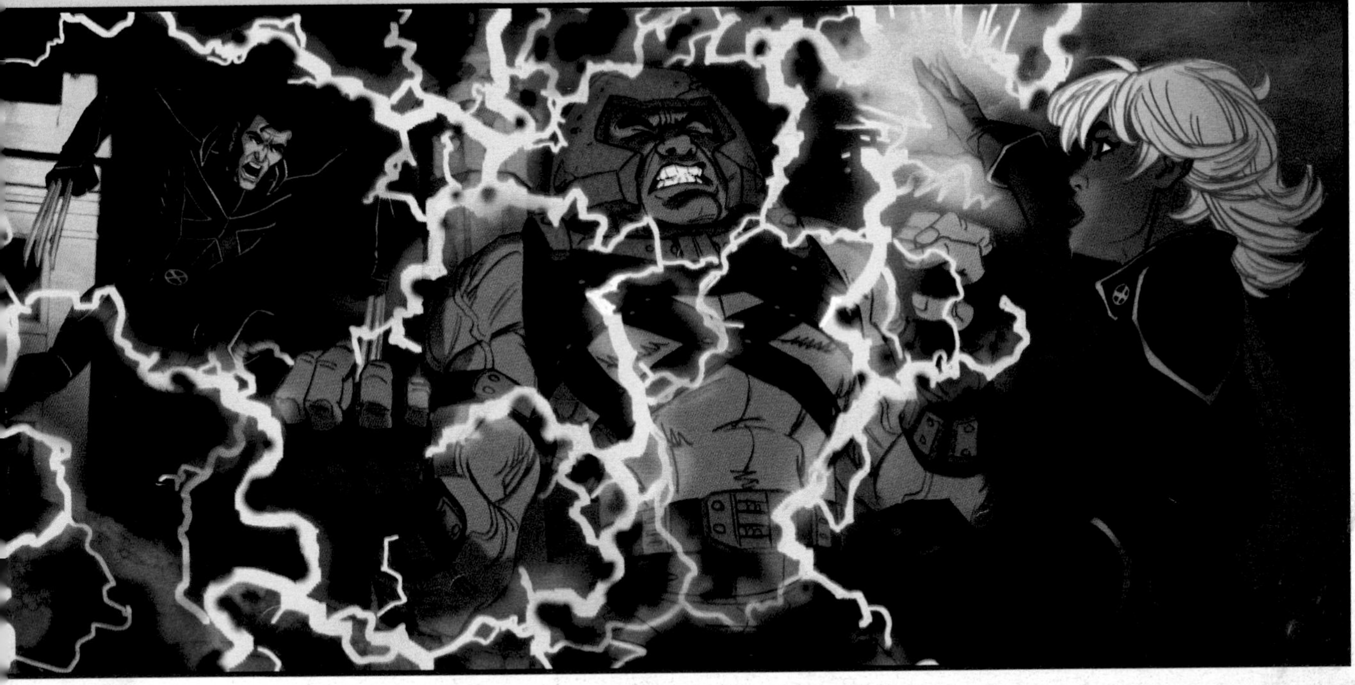

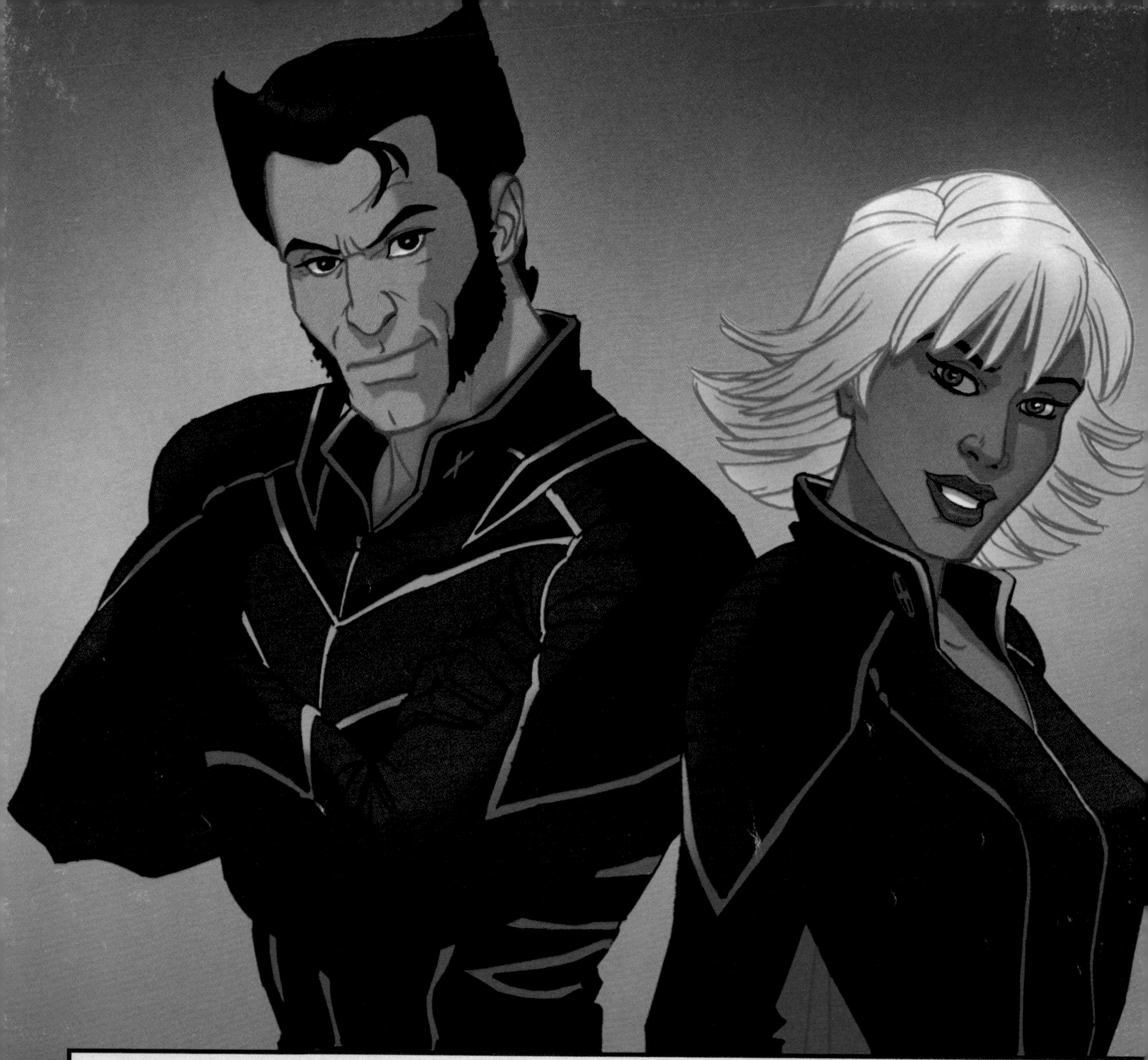

They weren't able to save Jean from her own dark powers. But the X-Men were able to defeat Magneto's forces, protect innocent human lives . . . and save the world once again.